God bless,

The Listening Book

The Soul Painting & Other Stories

James Webb

LIONESS
WRITING LIMITED

For Ruth, the best friend I've ever had.

"Stories are equipment for living."

Kenneth Burke

CONTENTS

ACKNOWLEDGMENTS

They say it takes a village to raise a child, and I think it probably takes a moderate-sized town to make a book a reality. Over the years many people have inspired, developed and encouraged me, and this book wouldn't have happened without them. I'd like to take the opportunity to thank my parents and family for their support, and Cheryl Johnson, Mrs. West and Peter Idris Taylor as representatives of those who have encouraged me over the years. I'm also grateful to Larry Crabb and the late Fred Craddock, for inspiration, and – of course – the brave men and women of Cornerstone Community in Australia (particularly, at this moment, Laurie and Pete). Finally, a big thank you to Mark and Elsa Lewis, who made this all possible.

There are many others, but they will have to wait for another book.

"Show me your ways..."

INTRODUCTION

Are you listening?

I hope so.

We can spend a lot of time concerned with whether or not God is paying any attention to us. It's probably better to spend that time being concerned about whether or not we're paying any attention to Him.

You see, God is speaking. He's always speaking. It was the first thing He did. What about us? Do we fill the silence with the sound of our own voice, or do we listen?

Do you know what God does when He has something really important that he wants to say to us? Do you know what miracle He performs; what amazing sign He uses? When God has something important to say to us, He tells us a story.

It works, doesn't it? Stories are a guaranteed way to get someone's attention. When you're talking to someone and their eyes are glazing over, looking this way and that for an escape route, try the line, "That reminds me of a story…" and see what happens.

The Bible itself is a story. An adventure story. A war story. A love story. Jesus never taught about the Kingdom of God without telling a story. Read the book of Acts and see how the early Church shared Jesus by using people's own stories. You see, stories aren't really about communicating facts. They're really about communicating a vision of how things could be. You just need to listen carefully. We shouldn't be surprised that such tiny things as stories can carry such a big vision. After all, when you put a shell no bigger than your hand to your ear, don't you hear the entirety of all the oceans?

So here are some stories. Read them and listen. This is not a place to find doctrine, but it may be a place to hear a still, small voice. This may not be a place to find answers, but it may be a place to have your curiosity aroused and to start you off on a life-changing quest. I can't guarantee that God will show up while you're reading them, but it may be a place for the Holy Spirit to confirm something that He has already been whispering to your heart. It may be a comfortable place. It may be an unsettling place. It may just be a place that brings a smile to your face. They are just stories after all. God does the heavy lifting, as long as we are paying attention.

So, pick up that shell and listen. Will you hear the sea, or just silence? Or maybe something else entirely...

The Soul Painting

There was once an Artist who believed in people. He believed that every single person who had ever lived had within them one great masterpiece, a Soul Painting, and he devoted his life to this belief. As an in-demand artist of considerable talent he could have committed himself to his work and lived in comfort for the rest of his days, but he rejected such things to travel, to be with people and to pass on the message of the Soul Painting.

One day the Artist met a woman whom no-one had ever believed in. She was enchanted by the Artist and his message of the Soul Painting. Although her wounds were still too fresh and raw for her to believe in herself, she dared to believe in his belief and began to paint. It took her many years but eventually she had finished her Soul Painting. It was strikingly beautiful, tragic and unique; one of the most amazing works of art that anyone had ever seen. During this time the woman had learned to love the Artist and his message and devoted the rest of her life to spreading the story of the Soul Painting. Wherever she went, people clamoured to see her. Many were amazed by her story, and many more captivated by her beautiful Soul Painting.

One of the men who heard her speak wanted more than anything to possess his own Soul Painting. He had heard her talk about the Artist and the beliefs which had led to her painting, but he was too afraid and intimidated by her amazing Soul Painting to pick up a paintbrush himself. "I could never paint anything as good as her," he told himself, torn between his desire and his doubt.

One day he had an idea and, at a time when no-one was watching, he took out his camera and snapped a good photo of the woman's Soul Painting. He took the camera home, printed out the biggest, best quality copy of the Soul Painting that he could afford and had it framed. He told his friends of the Artist and invited them to come and see his own Soul Painting. His friends visited his home and were awestruck and touched by the beautiful masterpiece on his wall. They too wanted their own Soul Painting. The man only knew of one way to pass on the magic of the Soul Painting, so he invited his friends to take their own photo of his photo and then it could be their own Soul Painting. His friends readily agreed, as it seemed like an easy way to get a masterpiece.

The friends took their photos home and showed their friends, who in turn asked to take a photo of the photo of the photo. They in turn invited their friends to take a photo of the photo of the photo of the photo, and so on it went. With each layer of photos, the detail and beauty of the original painting was distorted further and further until there was a crowd of individuals, each clutching photos showing nothing more than an ugly splodge of random colours. The beauty had been lost a long time ago.

Over time the number of people wanting to take photos declined. Every now and then another person would be convinced to take a photo of one of the photos, but whatever their motivation, it was now never because of the beauty of the Soul Painting.

One day the Artist will travel from town to town crying out, "Bring me your Soul Paintings," and he will be crowded by a mob of people waving grubby, crumpled photographs shouting, "Master, Master, look at my Soul Painting, my beautiful Soul Painting!" The Artist will look at them and say, "Get away from me. I never knew you."

Rufus and the Troll

No-one used the bridge any more. Instead they trekked the extra mile downstream to where the river was shallow enough to cross. People got wet, but at least they didn't get eaten. Everyone knew that the Troll who lived under the bridge was angry and mean and always hungry. Everyone would rather get wet.

Sometimes, in such times as this, everything changes because of someone who didn't know what everyone else knew. Or, perhaps, because of someone who knew what everyone else knew, but refused to accept it. One such person was the carpenter's young son, Rufus.

"Has anyone ever seen the Troll?" Rufus asked the townsfolk. They would look at one another, and no-one would speak.

"So how do you know there's a Troll under the bridge?" To Rufus, it seemed like the logical question to ask.

"I've heard him! I've been to the bridge and heard him, hollering and yelling and screaming. He told me that he was a Troll and he was going to eat me!" the baker spoke up, as the latest witness to the monster that lived under the bridge.

"But did you actually see him?" asked Rufus.

"Well…no," admitted the baker, "but if it screams that it's a Troll and that it's going to eat you, it's a Troll!"

"And it lives under a bridge," the butcher piped up, "which is where Trolls live. Everyone knows that."

"It's the plain facts," offered the baker.

"Hmmmmmm…"

Rufus was sceptical. The thing is, he had no real reason to be sceptical. The townsfolk were convinced, and he had to admit that if you took the evidence at face value then it seemed that they were right. Yet Rufus remained unsure. There was only one way to find out for certain. So, Rufus resolved that the next morning he would head out to the bridge and see for himself.

The sun rose and Rufus packed. The bridge was not far, so he was confident that he would arrive by mid-morning. He packed some cake and an apple so that he could sit by the river and eat if it turned out that there was no Troll after all, and he set out with his faithful dog, Parakletos, at his heel.

The bridge was further than he'd thought, and the sun was nearly at midpoint in the sky when he finally arrived. Parakletos barked with delight as he splashed in the river by the bank, and Rufus looked for a suitable place to sit and eat. His eyes were drawn, of course, to the crumbling, ivy-covered stone arch that formed the bridge over the river. No time like the present.

Rufus wondered down to the bridge and cleared his throat. A booming voice responded:

"I am the Troll who lives under the bridge, and I will eat you!"

Rufus was certainly taken aback and more than a little frightened by this declaration. His thoughts about cakes and apples were pushed aside and the idea of running away presented itself.

Thankfully, Rufus had not come alone. Parakletos was not dissuaded by the threat of being eaten. He scampered down to the bottom of the bridge and barked loudly.

"I am the Troll who lives under the bridge, and I will eat you!"

Parakletos barked louder.

"I SAID, I am the Troll who lives under the bridge, and I will eat you!"

Rufus knew something was up. Parakletos was by far the smartest dog in the village, and he was not one to hang around if there was even the slightest chance of being eaten. More likely, his fine nose had detected the smell of something other than Troll.

"Well," said Rufus, his courage returning, "you're going to have to eat me then." There was a prolonged silence, punctuated only by the sound of Parakletos barking.

"Really?" came the uncertain voice from under the bridge.

"Yes. Really."

"Oh…OK…well…ummmm…right then. I'll eat you."

"That's fine by me," said Rufus, though it certainly wasn't fine by him. Sometimes courage makes you call a bluff so that a greater wrong can be righted.

"Ummmm…it's just that…well, I've never eaten anyone before," the Troll explained.

"Oh?"

"Yes. To be honest, this is the longest anyone's ever stayed around. I'm not really sure what I'm supposed to do next."

"Why don't you come out? That would be a fine place to start," suggested Rufus, feeling a little sorry for the bridge-dweller.

The Troll crawled out from beneath the bridge, while Parakletos jumped up and down and barked. The Troll emerged, with white fluffy wool and a black, meek face.

"You're not a Troll!" exclaimed Rufus,

"Yes, I am! I'm a Troll! A mean, people-eating Troll! Baaaaaaa!"

"No, you're not a Troll. Unless I'm very much mistaken, you are a sheep."

"A sheep? Why would you say such a thing?"

"Because you are!" It seemed very clear to Rufus.

"Are you sure?" the 'Troll' asked.

"Very sure. I know the shepherd in our village. I play chess with him every Tuesday while he's watching the sheep. I have seen sheep at dawn and at dusk and from every conceivable angle. Well, almost every conceivable angle, and you are most certainly a sheep," Rufus said with a firm voice.

"Huh!" the 'Troll' seemed thoughtful. "Well, that would explain a few things…"

"Such as?"

"The wool, for starters. And the fact that deep down, if pushed you understand, really pushed, I would much rather eat some lovely green grass than a person," the 'Troll' admitted.

"So why are you telling everybody that you are a Troll?"

The 'Troll' seemed to be thinking hard.

"I remember one day coming to the river to get a drink, and I found a lovely place to drink in the shade under the bridge. Someone came along and I made a noise—"

"What kind of noise?"

"Well, now that you mention it, I suppose it was a kind of 'Baaaa'ing noise," the 'Troll' explained.

"I see." Rufus smirked, "Continue."

"So then someone said, 'What made that noise?' and someone else said, 'It came from under the bridge,' and someone else said, 'It's a Troll!' and they ran away. A Troll! So I looked around in terror, and I couldn't see anything, so I realised that they must be talking about me." The 'Troll' took a deep breath before continuing.

"Well, I was afraid to leave the bridge. If I was a Troll, then I should stay under the bridge. That's where Trolls belong. When people came to the bridge, I called out to them, and they all said the same thing, 'The Troll! There is a Troll under the bridge! Run away!' and they ran away. So, I came to the only logical conclusion, namely that I was a Troll and I should live under the bridge and behave accordingly," the 'Troll' concluded.

"I can definitely say that you are not a Troll. You are a sheep. If you don't believe me, have a look in the river. Look at your reflection. And Parakletos, you can stop barking now," Rufus said. Parakletos was not an obedient dog, but he was a clever one and that's nearly as good. He stopped barking.

The 'Troll' looked at his reflection in the crystal water and saw himself as Rufus saw him and as Parakletos had smelled him.

"Well I never…" the sheep said.

The villagers had said, 'If it lives under a bridge and threatens to eat people, it must be a Troll'.

Not always. Sometimes it's just a sheep who's been made to believe that he's a Troll.

14

Look on the Bright Side

The troubles started with the old man's cow. It got really sick, very suddenly. We all felt sorry for him. Things were hard and none of us could afford to lose an animal. The vet came out and wandered around the beast, looking and touching and measuring, and his conclusion was that it wasn't promising. I commiserated with the old man. "Looks bad," he admitted. "Tough loss," I replied. He looked at me and said, "There's always hope".

The cow died.

A little while after that we began watching the weather with concern. The clouds were full and black and the harvest was just around the corner. A pounding rain would be bad news for most of us. The old man had been around for a while, brought in a lot of harvests, so I asked him what he thought. "Looks bad," he agreed. "We're in trouble," I sighed. He looked and me and said, "There's always hope".

The heavy rain came and we suffered.

Some of us went hungry that season, but we made it through. All of us, except the old man's son, that is. The doctor came with a smile on his face, and left with grim and stony features. "What did he say?" I asked the old man. "Looks bad," the old man said. I didn't say anything else. He looked at me and said, "There's always hope."

His son died.

The rains continued. The dams were full, but so were the rivers. It wouldn't take much more for them to break their banks and then we'd all be in trouble, even the smart ones who had questioned the wisdom of settling in the foothills. I asked the old man if he'd ever seen anything like this. He admitted that he hadn't. "Looks bad," he nodded. I wondered aloud whether the storms would break before we did. He looked at me and said, "There's always hope."

The floods came. I drowned.

The first thing I did after I walked through the Pearly Gates was sit on a log next to Jesus and begin complaining. "The old man's crazy," I ranted, "Bad things just kept happening and he just refused to face up to it. He lived in denial of the truth. At first it was inspiring, but then it just became annoying."

I asked Jesus, "Do you think he'll ever realise that life is actually a bleak and difficult thing?"

Jesus looked at me and said, "There's always hope."

Mustard Seed

My hands were full, but the mustard seed looked so tempting. The man was giving them out for free, and how could I refuse a bargain like that? True, the seed did not look nearly so attractive as the precious gems that I was already carrying around. I could only carry so much, so I had to be discerning. I had already discarded everything but the most beautiful and valuable treasures, and I had hardly enough strength to carry even those.

But the seed was so small, and the man made it sound so good. And it was free. I was sure that I could make just a little space, just a little more space for the mustard seed. So, I jammed it in there, just between the sparkle and the shine of my treasures.

Years passed, and sometimes some of the treasure changed. I would exchange something I had for something that was even more valuable, and then on rare occasions I would exchange it back again. But the mustard seed I never gave away. It stayed there. It was so small that I always had room for it, and it did give me some comfort having it there. Like a lucky charm, it gave some peace and some calm in times when I needed it. The man had been right about that.

Then one day I met a man carrying nothing but a bush. He looked so out-of-place, so silly in the world in which I moved; the world of the valuable and the beautiful. I asked him about the bush.

"This grew from my mustard seed," he told me.

"I have a mustard seed too!" I said. "But it is just a seed, and always has been."

"I used to be like you," the man said, "my mustard seed didn't grow either. Then I realised that while my hands were full it couldn't grow. No room, you see. It needs space."

"But, that would mean letting go of my treasure!"

The man looked grim, as he nodded.

"But I wouldn't know where to begin. Which one should I put down first?"

"You can do it that way," the man agreed, "but it's better to let everything go at once. If you want the bush, you'll have to let it all go eventually."

Old Fool

There was once a small town in the midst of a drought-stricken land. In this town lived a man known to the locals as Old Fool. Every morning Old Fool would emerge from his ramshackle cabin dragging a pickaxe behind him, and he'd spend the day digging a hole. Under the harsh sun for years, his skin had become like cracked leather. His white hair and beard were permanently matted with red dust, and the same hard work that had bent his back double had given his limbs a wiry strength. If anyone ever asked him why he spent his days engaged in such back-breaking labour under the unforgiving glare of the sun, he would give the same answer that he had first given back when he was known as Young Fool. He would tell you that he had heard an Ancient Word which had told him that there was water under the ground, if you would just dig for it.

Every day some of the townsfolk would come and watch Old Fool hard at work, and get some amusement from throwing insults in his direction.

"I'm sure he'll break the drought any day now!"

"Maybe he forgot where he planted his crops!"

"Foolish redbeard!"

Every day Old Fool would dig and dig, and every evening he would return home even dryer than when he had left. After many years of his digging, the dust bowl was covered in pockets and craters, so many that from the sky it looked like the surface of the moon.

One day Old Fool was out carving the red soil with his pickaxe. As usual, a small crowd of those with nothing better to do had gathered to mock.

"I'm sure he'll break the drought any day now!"

"Maybe he forgot where he planted his crops!"

"Foolish redbeard!"

Old Fool has been doing this for so long the townsfolk had run out of new insults many years ago. On this morning, as on every other morning before, Old Fool ignored the insults and continued to dig. Just as the sun was reaching its highest point, the mockers were interrupted by a low and threatening rumble beneath their feet.

"What's that?"

"Feels like an earthquake!"

"Everybody run!"

But before a single soul could move, a huge and violent jet of water gushed forth from the hole that Old Fool was digging. It reached into the sky for at least a hundred metres before showering everything. The ground got wet. The townsfolk got wet. Old Fool got wet.

The topic of conversation changed abruptly. Old Fool didn't seem so foolish anymore.

"Well I never. He was right after all!"

"Did you see the water? He'll be rich! He'll never have to work again!"

"Well, I do remember telling you that we should be nicer to him…"

The next morning the townsfolk gathered in great numbers to see Old Fool's geyser. The water had continued gushing forth all through the night, and the townsfolk were amazed to see that the holes that Old Fool had dug throughout the years had become pools and ponds, full of fresh life-giving water. Then the door to Old Fool's cabin opened, and out came Old Fool dragging his trusty pickaxe behind him. He nodded at the townsfolk, then turned and walked off towards the dry and dusty distance.

"What's he doing?"

"He's still digging? Even after yesterday?"

"I told you he'd still be Old Fool."

Many months passed. The water that Old Fool had found continued to flow, and the countryside that he had been digging in had become lush and green. Flowers grew, animals grazed and people came from miles around to drink. Yet Old Fool continued to head off alone each morning, carrying his pickaxe into the desert to keep digging.

One day some of the townsfolk followed him to ask him why he kept going. "Why do you keep digging? You've found water. You don't need to dig anymore."

Old Fool glared at them and replied, "Your mistake is in thinking that I was digging for my own benefit. I was digging so that others could drink." The townsfolk shook their heads, shrugged their shoulders and walked off. They did not understand.

Soon after this, Old Fool died and was buried in the dust bowl where he had spent his life digging. His grave is a nondescript plot of dirt in the middle of nowhere, marked only by a headstone that has been crudely formed from a large boulder. People continue to visit his oasis, but no-one bothers to visit his grave. If you ask the townsfolk, not one of them can tell you who buried him or who placed his headstone there. But if you ask, a few of them might be able to tell you what has been engraved on it. An Ancient Word. "His labour was not in vain".

Tame the Sun

Despite his frustrations, the man was ultimately in favour of the sun. After all, it provided a lot of good things for him. It kept him warm and gave light for him see by. He gathered that it did the same things for a lot of other people too. More than that, he understood that actually the whole planet benefited from the presence of the sun. It was not just him, or even all the people, but also plants, animals and the entire ecosystem. With all that in mind, it was hard not to be pro-sun. He would tell anyone who listened about the benefits of the sun, but there was always a tinge of annoyance inside him when he did so. The sun was all well and good during the daytime, but he felt it was rather remiss of it to allow the dark of the night to fall. As far as he could tell, night and the feeble moon served no purpose — at least, not compared to the sun. In fact, the night seemed like a total missed opportunity to him. All he ever did was sleep, which seemed like a rather inefficient use of his time. And it wasn't as if him sleeping let the sun off the hook. He could sleep in the sun if he wanted. He'd probably enjoy it more. He'd be warmer, for one thing, and save a lot of money on heating bills. And if he woke up needing a drink, he wouldn't need to turn on the light to see his way to the kitchen. The sun's refusal to accept a 24-hour contract seemed, to him, nothing more than selfish and just plain lazy.

So, the man decided that what he needed to do was insist rather strongly that the sun amend its routine and play by his rules. Things would work out better if the sun followed his schedule, rather than vice versa. In fact, as far as he could tell, the only ones who stood to lose out were the bats and the owls. But who cares about bats and owls anyway?

The man decided to begin by standing in a field at noon and delivering an impassioned plea to the great yellow eye above him. To his disappointment, when the allocated time arrived, the sun vanished behind the horizon and its pathetic cousin, the moon, rose as normal. Perhaps the sun had not been able to hear him?

The man had friends in highish places, so he consulted with his allies at NASA and arranged for his speech to be delivered over radio waves, sent into the very heart of the sun. On a loop. Twenty four times should do it, he thought, one for every hour of the day. And so it happened. His convincing arguments were transmitted across space, but once more, as the evening arrived, the sun bid goodbye for the day and handed over to its lunar understudy.

The man had moved beyond frustration. He was now angry. There was no way that the sun had not heard his speech, and yet it remained unmoved. Literally. This just confirmed his opinion, that the sun was egocentric; that ultimately it believed that it was the centre of the universe, or at least, the centre of the solar system. Drastic times called for drastic measures.

The man decided that there was only one option left to him. He must go himself and present his case to the sun, face-to-face. The man once more spoke with the powers-that-be at NASA and they arranged for a rocket to be sent to the sun. The man would be on that rocket, with a new speech prepared. A declaration of war, if you will. This time there would be a result in his favour, because this time the sun would not be answering to his voice, or to radio waves. This time the sun would be answering to him.

Of course, the rocket burst into flames before it even got to Mercury's orbit, and everything and everyone within it was incinerated. This included the man, and his pre-prepared speech.

And so it goes for all those who respond to grace with entitlement.

The Note

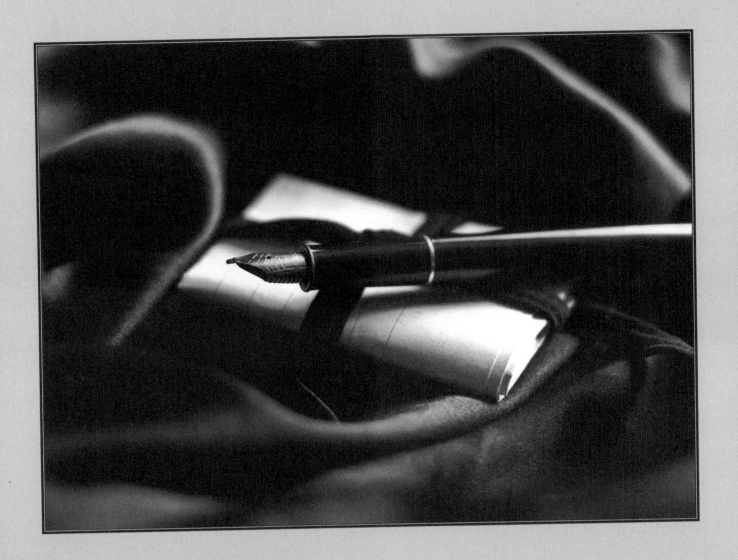

I remember when I sat with my friend, when he found out that his girlfriend had decided that it wasn't working out and it was time for her to move on. I remember his look of pain; the pain that can only come from allowing another to have possession of your heart. I remember the tears welling up in his eyes. I remember stammering over my words, unsure what to offer. And then I remember, clear as day, him slowly reaching into his pocket and pulling out a folded piece of paper. I remember the slow deliberate action as he opened it up. It was not a big piece of paper, no bigger than a page from a notebook. I remember him studying it intensely, as though it contained the secret of all things. Then I remember him folding it up just as deliberately as he had unfolded it, and returning it to its home in his pocket. I remember him smiling at me through the tears in his eyes; the smile of one who knows that the wound, though excruciating, will not be fatal.

At first I thought that folded paper was a note from his former girlfriend. Something to remember her by - "I'm sorry. I didn't deserve you" - something like that. But I remember the next time that I saw him take out the note, when he had just been informed of his brother's death. I saw him draw out the scrap of paper again, and study it as before. I saw him return it to his pocket, and the smile was there. Not the smile of humour, but rather the smile of one who has decided to choose joy even in the midst of suffering.

I was there when he found out that he had lost his job. Again, the note. Again, the look of calm acceptance.

I was there when the rumours began, except I won't call them rumours. The proper name for them was 'lies'. Misunderstood and spoken of unfairly, the note seemed to offer comfort once more.

Every time I saw him suffer, I saw the note. I can only assume that the note was also there even when I was not. Over the years, there was no doubt that my friend changed. Suffering changes people. Some of them stare into the face of pain and become hard, like those who stared into the face of Medusa. Their outer shell becomes unyielding and smooth, but inside the soft bitterness and resentment curdles the soul. Then there are the others, who see something else in the face of suffering. Acquainted with hardship, their wisdom and love grows in direct proportion. These others become loved themselves, because there is something irresistibly attractive about those who refuse to be harmed by the slings and arrows of both outrageous fortune and deliberate attack. My friend, he was one of these others. The note, whatever it said, had reminded him of whatever he needed to be reminded of for this transformation to occur.

The final time that I was there was when he found out the results of the test; the unspeakable C word. Not long to go now. The note, now dog-eared and worn from the years, once more. Again, the contagious peace.

He lay in the hospital bed, measuring his life in hours, when he spoke to me.

"I want you to have something."

He passed me the note, folded and warm. I took it, but said nothing. Words seemed inadequate.

"One thing. Don't read it until you really need to."

So the note remained in my pocket, unlooked at, until the day of the funeral. I sat there in the church, filled with mourners; part of a non-stop parade of memories. One person spoke. Then another. And another. Each told a different story, but the punchline was always the same. This man, who knew suffering, was a rock against whom others leaned when their own strength failed them. I wept. I missed my friend, and I needed him. I needed his calming, unshakable presence in my life. No, not just me. The world needed him. So many touched by so short a life. I had seen him cry countless times and I was now ashamed that he had never once seen me cry. So I cried now, and cursed the arbitrary nature of the universe.

Now was the time, I realised. The time of need. I reached into my pocket, and slowly, reverently, I pulled the note free. It sat there in my hand for seconds, unopened. I stared at it, wondering about its secret, oblivious to the hymn being sung by the crowd around me. One fold. Two folds. A third fold, and the note lay open before me. I looked down at the scrawled script and read the words that had changed my friend's life, and consequently changed the lives of others. Just five words: "Remember that life isn't fair."

Urges to be Killed (One)

The guards brought the Stranger before my throne.

"My lord, may your name be ever praised, we found this person stirring up the peasants by demanding the destruction of your city," the grovelling guards stuttered as they shuffled back from the prisoner.

"Well?" I said, eyeing the nondescript Stranger up and down. "What do you have to say for yourself?"

"Nice place you've got here," he responded, "but it has to fall."

"Guards," I said, before pausing for dramatic effect. "Kill him."

The guards grabbed the Stranger and pulled him from my presence. The Stranger looked at me, and as he was led from the throne room, he just smiled.

***

The next morning the guards brought the Stranger before me again.

"My lord, may your name—" the guards began, but I raised my hand and they fell silent. At least they had the decency to look embarrassed.

"I thought I'd had you killed," I said to the Stranger.

"I've been dead before," he replied, "but I didn't much care for it."

"And so you've come back?"

"This city must fall," he stated plainly.

"This city will never fall. I know this. I built it myself with my own hands. I dug the foundations. I laid each brick. It is solid. It is magnificent. It is a testament to my ability, my leadership, my self-sufficiency."

"And that is exactly why it must fall." The Stranger glared at me.

39

"Guards. Take him away and kill him. And do it properly this time." I waved my hand nonchalantly. Inside I was anything but nonchalant. No-one spoke to me this way, not in my city.

Once more the guards led the Stranger from my throne room. Once more he just smiled.

***

The next morning the Stranger approached my throne again. The guards did not bring him this time. He came alone, of his own accord.

"Why won't you stay dead?" I barked.

"Because this is important," his firm reply.

"You will not destroy my city!" I brought my fist down on the arm of my throne.

"Me? I can't destroy it. You said it yourself. It's 'your city'. You're the only one who can destroy it. And that's exactly what you must do."

"You cannot tell me what I must do! I am king here, lord and protector of my people—"

"Your people?" the Stranger interrupted. "Take a look at your people. Take a *proper* look at your people." His tone discouraged disobedience.

So I looked at the guards in the throne room. I looked hard. I rose from my throne and went to the window. I looked at the peasants, milling around below me like worker ants. I looked hard. I saw my people as they really were - pale, washed-out phantoms. Each one made in my image, and my image alone. Unbidden, a single tear rolled down my cheek.

"Nothing here is real," the Stranger announced, "not really. Either the city falls, or you do. But mark my words, something will fall."

"But this city is my greatest achievement. Who am I without it?" I was almost pleading with him. I couldn't help myself.

"This is the last time I will come to you. Choose."

I closed my eyes and I made my choice. A rumble began deep below me. The ground immediately became unsteady beneath my feet. A terrible sound caused me to open my eyes, and I saw my throne split in two as through a huge axe had crashed down on it. The destruction, which had begun with my throne, spread like spilt milk to the stone floor and then the walls. Everywhere I turned I saw decay, and at my feet a gaping chasm, both horrifying and inviting. I screamed as I fell, and the darkness took me.

And the Stranger? He just smiled.

Flowers and Weeds

The boy found a seed. He didn't know what kind of a seed it was. He was just a boy. But even the boy knew that seeds were made to be planted, so that is what he did. He buried it in the earth and attended to it. He watered it every day, each time looking and praying and hoping to see a shoot pushing its way out of its earthy coffin. Just a boy, and he loved that flower-to-be as only a boy could.

One day, to his delight, a green shoot, peeping out at him. The boy learned a lesson that day. Faith and love were always rewarded. He nurtured that young plant like a mother until it blossomed into a beautiful yellow flower. It was not the biggest flower, nor the prettiest, but to that boy it was wondrous and – more importantly – it was his.

Then his parents took him to one side to educate him. The plant was a dandelion. A dandelion was not a flower. It was a weed. The boy had grown a weed. He was heart-broken. The boy walked away from the plant and never looked back. He had showered his affection on something that was merely a weed disguised as a flower. It was no longer beautiful. A useless, dirty weed. He was ashamed of its ugliness and of his stupidity. The boy learned another lesson, but this one tasted bitter.

The Lesson: There is nothing more foul-tasting than to be disappointed; to find that the flower you had invested yourself in was actually a weed. It is better not to care. It is better not to love unless you are absolutely certain, one-hundred-percent convinced that the seed is that of a rose. Beware, lest you pour yourself into something or someone useless. Beware, weeds masquerading as flowers.

The boy walked away that day. Do not judge him too harshly. He was only a boy, after all. I hope that when he becomes a man he may see things differently. That he may see things the same way as the wrinkled, wizened Albanian nun who saw the face of Christ in the poorest, ugliest beggars. Who saw a flower in every weed.

I pray that when he becomes a man he may see things differently. That he may see things the same way as the wandering, preaching carpenter who said, "Whatever you do for the least of these weeds, you do for me."

I am sure that when he becomes a man he will see things differently. He will be taken by the hand, led into the garden and spoken to: "You see all these faces, all these spectacular flowers? They were weeds that somebody loved."

The Boy who Held God

The boy walked down the street, hands shoved into his pockets, whistling a nameless tune as he strolled. His path took him past the foreboding church on the corner. Outside the front of the church was a large wooden noticeboard, on which were printed three bold words. The boy's mind, being essentially a sponge, absorbed the words without his consent, but the new information pulsed along networks and, as the boy became aware, his pace slowed and the whistling died on his lips. The words on the noticeboard, in loud black font:

GOD IS EVERYWHERE

The boy stopped. He read the words. He looked around. He read the words again.

GOD IS EVERYWHERE

He pulled his hands out of his pockets, and gazed down at one of them, palm outstretched. He read the words once more. He thought. He stared at his palm. Then he smiled, and closed his fingers into a chubby little fist. "Everywhere…" he whispered to himself. Then he returned his remaining hand to its pocketed home, and continued on his way, whistled tune and clenched hand accompanying him.

When the boy arrived home his transformation went – at first – unnoticed. If one had paid attention to the way that he whistled, or his swagger, or simply the look in his eyes then one would have become aware that something magnificent had happened to this child. As it was, his parents did not notice the change that had come upon him until it was time for dinner. And they noticed not because of the lightness in his step or the smile on his lips, but rather because he was trying to eat his chips and beans with a fork jammed awkwardly in between the fingers of his clenched fist.

"My goodness, why are you eating like that, dear?" asked his curious Mother.

"God is everywhere," the boy declared through mangled chips and beans, waving his closed fist triumphantly.

Mother's heart skipped a beat, but only because as he waved his fist a single bean plopped from his fork on to the clean tablecloth.

"Be careful, dear, and what do you mean 'God is everywhere'?"

"God is everywhere," the boy repeated, again holding up his fist.

"Oh, I see…and you think that you have God there, in your hand?" Mother enquired.

The boy carried on eating. The obvious needs no confirmation.

"How adorable," purred Mother, glancing at Father on the other side of the table, who merely peered at her over the top of his newspaper, eyebrows raised.

Different parents make different mistakes, but if parents throughout time and space all have one common flaw, it's that they frequently underestimate the conviction of their children. As the days passed and the boy's fist remained clenched, 'adorable' became 'annoying', which as anyone knows, is just one short step from 'concerning' for most parents, and once you reach 'concerning' things tend to snowball at an alarming rate until you are right smack in the middle of 'distressing'. A phone call was made to the school, who informed the worried Mother that they were aware of the problem, and that measures were being taken.

Later that day, at school, the class was gathered while the teacher provided education on the subject of hygiene. It had, in discussion with the headmaster, been deemed an appropriate topic by which to address the critical issue.

"—and that," the teacher explained, "is why it's crucial to wash your hands. And on that matter, I have a question for one of you." He gestured in the direction of the boy. "Why do you have your hand closed up like that? It's been weeks since anyone has seen your palm. I would imagine that it's most unhygienic."

"God is everywhere." The boy grinned, as he held out his fist.

"Is that why you've had your hand closed for so long? Because you think that you have God in…oh dear," the teacher said as he shook his head. He couldn't recall ever coming across such an advanced and debilitating case of superstition before.

"Now, class," the teacher spoke to the group, but his eyes were locked on the smiling child with the dirty fist. "Very often, two people can see the same thing and draw radically different conclusions. Thankfully, in this case, there is a very simple way to see which of us is right." He spoke now to the boy, "Open your hand."

The boy hesitated.

"Just open your hand. If God is everywhere, and you are holding Him, then if you open your hand, we should see Him. Correct?"

The boy held out his palm and began, slowly, to uncurl the fingers that had been clenched tight for days. Each student in the class leant over their desk, with baited breath, desperate to see what would be revealed in the open hand.

"What do you see?" the teacher asked.

The boy stared down at his empty palm.

"I see…nothing," he said, and burst into tears.

The teacher sighed. He was not an unkind man, but this was something that needed to be done. He gripped the chalk tightly in his hand and scrawled on the blackboard:

GOD IS NOWHERE.

"Class. What does this say?"

"God is nowhere," intoned the group, minus one tiny, sobbing voice.

At that moment, the bell for lunch rang. The class filled with energy, and children rapidly filed out of the room, chattering and wondering what delights their lunch boxes would hold for them today. They gave no further thought to the boy, his empty hand or the idea that God is everywhere. They had already moved on. No-one paid any notice to the boy, still sitting at his desk, weeping.

The teacher, as he moved past, paused long enough to gently pat the boy on the shoulder.

"It gets easier with time," he assured, and then he left the room. As mentioned before, he was not an unkind man.

The boy, alone with the nowhere God, looked up and focussed on the words. He dragged his arm across his red eyes.

The boy stopped crying. He read the words. He looked around. He read the words again.

GOD IS NOWHERE.

He gazed down at his outstretched, empty palm. He read the words once more. He thought. He stared at his palm. His teacher had been right. Very often two people will see the same thing and draw radically different conclusions.

He stood up and made his way to the board. He picked up a piece of chalk and with the tip of his finger he swept away one of the letters. Then, in his crude scrawl, he put the letter back, having added nothing more than a little space. He looked at what he had written, and smiled.

GOD IS NOW HERE.

The boy put his hands into his pockets, and strolled out of the classroom, whistling as he went.

Meanwhile, God looked down into His palm and smiled.

The Sister and the King

The sun set on the battlefield, the ground soaked with red. One hundred had fallen that day, and somewhere, many miles away, a sister's heart broke.

Word reached her that her brother and the others who died were to be buried on the field, their graves a monument to duty. But to the sister, this would not do. Her brother, noble and courageous, deserved better. So she began a journey to the capital, to petition the King and have her brother honoured as he deserved.

She was not long on the road when she came across a woodcutter. Beside the road he chopped and chopped, but as she approached he halted his work.

"Hello there, sister. Where do you go and why?"

"I am going to the capital to petition the King, to have my brother honoured in death with the honour that he showed in life."

"Your brother? A tall, noble-looking fellow with golden hair? A man whose gentle hands bore the scars of both battle and work?"

"Yes. That was him."

"He passed by on his way to the battle. As he passed I injured my hand. He not only stopped to tend to my wound, but stayed to finish my day's work. A truly great man."

"You speak kindly of my brother, gentle woodcutter. Would you accompany me on my journey and add your voice to my petition? The King will surely listen if there are two of us."

"Sister, I would be delighted to do this."

So, the sister and the woodcutter continued their journey towards the capital. With the woodcutter by her side the sister felt certain that her petition would be heard.

They were not much further down the road when they came across a beggar. Beside the road he sat and asked for money, but as they approached he stopped his begging.

"Hello there, sister. Where do you go and why?"

"I am going to petition the King, to have my brother honoured in death with the honour that he showed in life."

"Your brother? A tall, kindly-faced fellow with golden hair? A man whose honest eyes saw both the detail and the whole?"

"Yes. That was him."

"He passed by on his way to the battle. As he passed he stopped and gave me his money. Not only this, he also gave me all of his food and water. A truly great man."

"You speak kindly of my brother, gentle beggar. Would you accompany us on our journey and add your voice to our petition? The King will surely listen if there are three of us."

"Sister, I would be delighted to do this."

So, the sister, the woodcutter and the beggar continued their journey towards the capital. With the woodcutter and beggar by her side the sister felt certain that her petition would be heard.

They were not much further down the road when they came across a scholar. Beside the road he sat and read a book, but as they approached he lowered his tome.

"Hello there, sister. Where do you go and why?"

"I am going to petition the King, to have my brother honoured in death with the honour that he showed in life."

"Your brother? A tall, lion-hearted fellow with golden hair? A man whose clear voice was suited to both song and command?"

"Yes. That was him."

"He passed by on his way to the battle. As he passed he stopped and spoke with me for a while. We spoke of philosophy and science and I was educated by his wisdom. A truly great man."

"You speak kindly of my brother, gentle scholar. Would you accompany us on our journey and add your voice to our petition? The King will surely listen if there are four of us."

"Sister, I would be delighted to do this."

So, the sister, the woodcutter, the beggar and the scholar continued their journey towards the capital. With the woodcutter, beggar and scholar by her side the sister felt certain that her petition would be heard.

And so it came to pass that the party arrived at the capital and sought an audience with the King.

Word had already arrived of the strange group and their quest, and they were soon admitted into the King's court.

In the presence of the King, the sister almost lost her nerve, but she recalled to memory her brother and she did not falter. Sister, woodcutter, beggar and scholar all bowed low before the King and then she spoke:

"Great and mighty King. My brother fought and died in your name. I have come to ask that he might be honoured amongst those who fell. For as great as your army is, I am sure that there are few amongst its ranks that loved you as much and served you as well. My companions will bear witness to his chivalry, and add their voices to mine."

The King looked at the sister with sympathy, and replied, "Child, I do not doubt your brother's character, and that will not be forgotten, but it would be wrong to give him greater honour than the other ninety nine. For all those men served, all those men did their duty that day and all those men made the same sacrifice for me. You see one through the eyes of his sister, but I see one hundred through the eyes of their King."

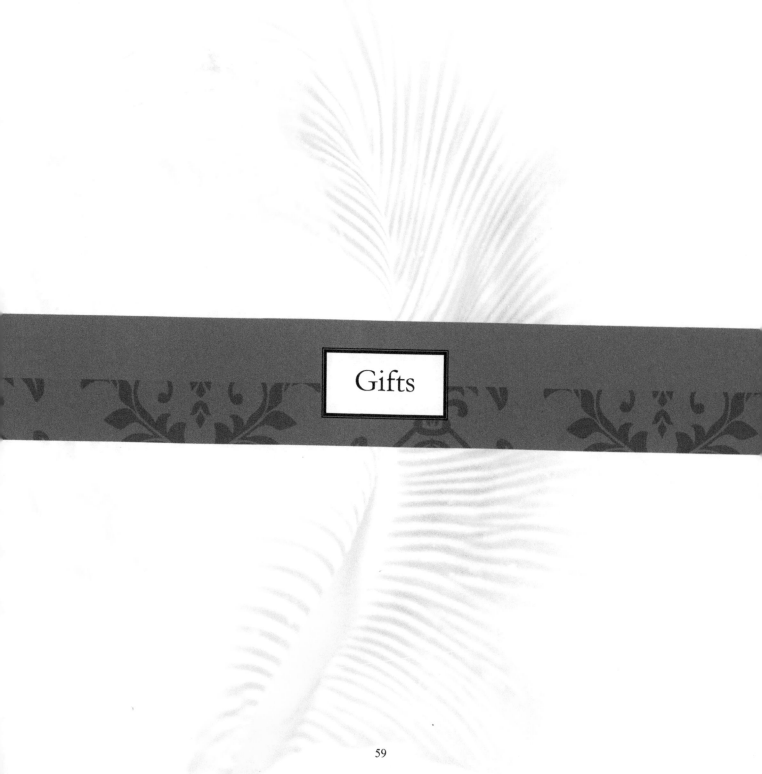

Gifts

I remember the day well. There was a knock at the door. I opened it and there was God, just standing there. He held something out to me. It sparkled brightly.

"This is for you," he said.

"What is it?" I asked.

"A gift."

I took it. It was heavy! I remember that well. It took both hands to carry it. I heaved this thing into the living room and placed it there on the mantelpiece. Pride of place, of course. It was my gift, given to me by God himself. I loved having it there. It reminded me of Him, you see. I would get up in the morning and get ready for the day, and I would come downstairs and see it there every day, sparkling and shining. It reminded me of God, and it reminded me of how much He loved me.

When friends came over, I would show them my gift. They would admire it. Sometimes, when I went to their houses, I would see their gifts too. They had them framed or mounted or put in a display case. They were all unique, all so different, but they had two things in common. One, they all sparkled like a star, and two, they were all very heavy.

One day, I saw a man stumbling along the road. He had a rucksack on his back, and he was obviously struggling with it. Even from a distance I could see the sparkle and I knew that he had his gift, right there in the rucksack. I spoke to him as he approached.

"I know what's in there. Why are you carrying it around like that?"

"I have to do this. Otherwise I might forget," he responded.

"Forget what?" I asked.

"That a gift is supposed to be a burden."

Treasure

I used to go to this big church. It was really good, you know? The music was great and the pastor was pretty good too. He could preach up a storm when he wanted to, but sometimes he went on a bit too long. One day the pastor resigned and left the church. He said he'd had enough and that he couldn't take it anymore, but no-one was quite sure what the 'it' was. We just looked at one another and nodded. Another one bites the dust. Christian leadership seems to attract some of these weaker types who can't handle the pressures of a real job. So he left the church and retired to live in a cottage by himself in the middle of nowhere. We forgave him for letting us down, but he really shouldn't have done it. It's like that thing that Jesus said: "If you can't stand the heat, don't go into the kitchen in the first place."

Anyway, we heard that he'd moved into his little cottage and was getting on quite fine, but that one day he'd been digging in the garden and he'd struck oil. Can you believe that? He was digging in a flower bed or something and WHOOSH! this huge gush of black gold just rushed out of the ground. Well, suddenly he had more money than he knew what to do with. A few of us who were still at the church thought it would be a good idea to just remind him who his friends were, if you know what I mean. It would be wrong to say that we felt that he owed us something, but he did really. He'd abandoned us.

Some of his old congregation wrote him letters or phoned him, reminding him of a few facts. We gave you a house, and paid you a good wage, and put up with your strange habits and long sermons. It's only fair that you share some of your blessings with us, just as we did with you. It's like that thing that Paul said in Acts: "It is better that you give to me than I give you anything." That didn't seem to do the trick though. A few others thought it was only right to be honest and up front, so they wrote him letters and phoned him to ask him for money. I mean, you can't be more transparent than that – and that's the Christian thing to do, isn't it? How could he say no to that? I don't know, but he did. He just laughed and hung up the phone. Can you understand that? I thought he was supposed to be a Christian.

Anyway, a few of us smarter ones realised that nothing does the trick like a bit of flattery, so we decided to try that approach. One of my friends got all the recordings of the pastor's sermons and put them up on the internet. It took him hours. He e-mailed the pastor the link to the site, but he never visited it. Someone else suggested that we put a plaque up in the church, honouring the pastor for his service. I went one better than that and wrote the guy a letter, telling him how much I'd grown because of his preaching and example, and that I saw Christ in him and all that kind of stuff. And what happened? Nothing. We went to all this trouble and he didn't even send us a single penny. Have you ever experienced such ingratitude? We hadn't. We were shocked and, frankly, appalled that this man had led us for so many years. We'd thought he was a good guy, you know?

A little later we heard that the pastor died. We got a bit excited, because maybe he'd left us something in his will. That would explain everything! He was waiting until he'd died to give us what we were owed. A small group of us went to a bit of trouble so that we could attend his funeral and hear the reading of the will. So we sat through the funeral, barely able to contain our anticipation, and after the wake, we all funnelled into the lawyer's office to find out the contents of the will. The lawyer took one look at us and said, "I've got some bad news." I don't know why we were surprised. We shouldn't have been, bearing in mind everything that had gone before, but we were. Of course he'd left us nothing. Apparently he'd died a poor man, having already given away all his wealth to various charities and good causes.

You have no idea how angry it made us to have to sit and listen to the list of people he had given his money away to when we hadn't seen any of it. It was so unfair! We grumbled and stamped our feet, and got up to leave, but then the lawyer said, "Wait! He did leave something to one of you. He left his most prized possession, something that was too precious to him for him to give away until after he died. Something that he had kept close to him through his final days." Well, that stopped us in our tracks. Who had he left it to? What was it? The lawyer just held up his hand to stop our questions, and then he pointed at me. Me! That's right! He'd left his most prized possession to me. I was so pleased and so proud, and the others who had come with me looked at me and told me not to forget who my friends were. I reminded them that some people are generous by nature and not to worry. I would set the example that the pastor should have done.

Then the lawyer brought out a big wooden chest and gave it to me. It was so heavy and so big! It barely fit into the boot of my car, but I squeezed it in and drove home imagining what could be in it. Money? Jewels? Gold bullion? As soon as I got home I dragged the chest from my car and took it into the garage to open it. But I couldn't open it. It was locked with a big, tough padlock and the lawyer hadn't seen fit to give me the key. I hammered the chest with my fists, and kicked it, and screamed and shouted at it to open, but it didn't budge. Then I had an idea. I went into my shed and grabbed a sledgehammer and took it back to the garage. Then I smashed that padlock with the hammer just as hard as I could. It didn't even make a mark. I hammered it again. Not a scratch. I tried a third time, and nothing. I was just about to give up, when I realised that the chest might be easier to break than the padlock. It was big and heavy, sure, but it was also old. So I swung again and bashed the chest. There was a splintering sound which filled me with joy. I bashed again and this time a big hole appeared in the top of the chest. Finally, a third time and SMASH! the top of the chest flew apart so that I could see what was inside and get what I deserved. With expectation and a sense of thrill I peered inside. The pastor's chest was empty, except for the letter that I'd written to him.

Mirror Mirror

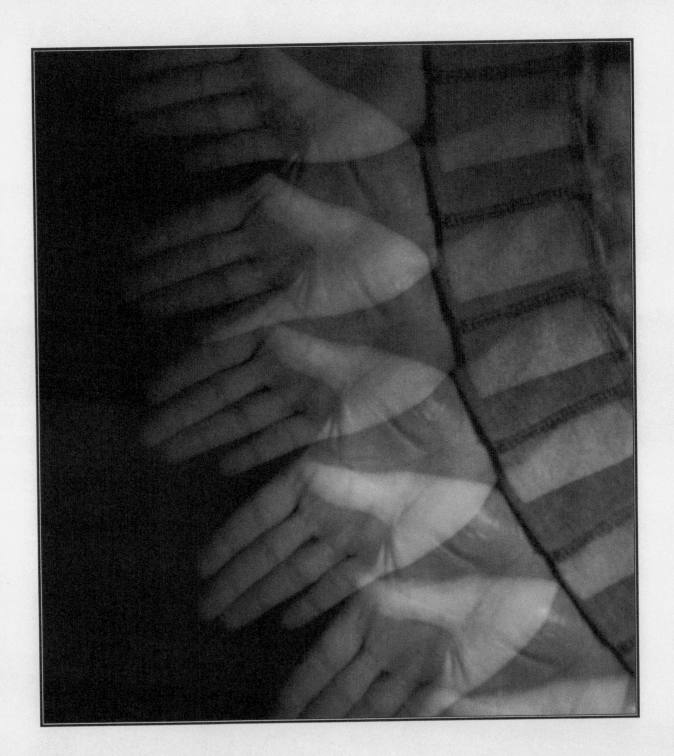

There was once a man who was committed to improving himself. He moved in a world of people who had, long ago, given up on trying to grow and mature, but he had decided to walk a harder path. He wanted to become more than he was, and he knew that this was not only a noble goal, but also the true path to happiness.

His quest would have been much harder if it were not for the Mirror. The Mirror helped him. When he looked at his reflection, he was able to see his faults and flaws, the things about him that stopped him from becoming the man that he wanted to be. Once he had been shown a rough edge, he would sit with his friends and talk with them. Together they would decide the best way to overcome the weakness. The Mirror showed him the fault, but it was his friends who helped him to beat it. He relied on them, but they relied on him too, for they all had their own Mirrors, and pursued the same goal for themselves.

As time went on, the man changed for the better. He began to feel pleased with himself, perhaps even proud. He started to notice things in his friends, weaknesses that they had not yet seen in their Mirrors. His impatience with them began to take root. He was outgrowing them, he decided. They were not mature enough to help him anymore. He didn't need them. He had his Mirror, and together they could solve whatever problems he had. So he stopped meeting with his friends, and decided that between himself and the Mirror, his needs would be met and his growth assured.

But, over time, he noticed that his Mirror was getting smaller and smaller until, one day, it was gone altogether. The man stopped becoming more than he was. He became something else entirely.

On the Perils of Having a High Estimation of Artistic Talent

It was a beautiful day; a perfect day to bake a loaf of bread. On days like this, mused Edith, there was nothing more wonderful than sitting in the sun with a thick layer of butter spread on a slice of home-made bread.

The loaf was duly baked and placed on a window ledge to cool a little, and Edith went to her pantry to locate the slab of butter that she could hardly wait to introduce to the freshly-baked bread.

On returning to the kitchen, she was greeted by a most unwelcome sight. Her loaf, her precious perfect loaf, had been torn and gouged and reduced to a pile of chunky crumbs. Amidst the carnage sat the culprit: a big, fat blackbird, flapping its wings and gulping down her bread.

SPLAT! went the butter as it fell to the kitchen floor and SQUAWK! went the blackbird as Edith grabbed it by its chubby neck.

"My bread! You've ruined my bread!" she squawked herself.

"I'm sorry! I'm sorry!" gasped the blackbird, "it was an accident!"

"An accident! An accident! How—" Edith began, but she stopped. The blackbird had started singing.

Edith gasped. Such a beautiful, haunting melody, unlike anything she had ever heard before, from beast or man. She would not have expected this from anything, let alone the winged vandal that had just destroyed her own work of art. A tear of appreciation ran down Edith's cheek, and she released her grip on the blackbird.

"Surely anyone that could produce such beautiful music can't be all bad," she admitted, as the bird arched its way higher and higher into the sky.

So, back to the drawing board. The dough was made, kneaded and shaped. The oven heated and the loaf cooked. When the smell of freshly-baked bread permeated the house, Edith removed the loaf from the oven and placed it once more on the window sill. As it cooled, she attempted to salvage what she could of her floor butter.

Deep in thought, Edith didn't hear the subtle flapping of wings outside the window. Consumed by her task, she didn't notice the sound of clawed feet perching on warm crust. She did, however, become aware that something was wrong when she was suddenly showered with small crumbs. Up like a shot, she was greeted by another gruesome crime scene. The blackbird had returned and was violating her loaf once more.

"That is enough!" she screamed, and grabbed the plump bird once again.

"No! I'm sorry! I'm sorry!" the blackbird squawked again.

"Do you think I'm stupid? What do you—" Edith began, but the words faded once more. Again, the blackbird had begun to sing.

She had forgotten just how sublime the blackbird's voice was. Each note lingered in her memory like a particularly bittersweet snapshot from her childhood. Her resolve wavered.

"Do you promise to leave my bread alone?" she asked the bird.

"I promise! I promise!" the blackbird assured her.

"Very well then," Edith said, and released the feathered miscreant.

"Surely anyone that could produce such beautiful music can't be all bad," she repeated, as she watched the blackbird soar higher and higher.

A third loaf was mixed and baked, and once more placed on the window sill to cool. At first Edith had thought about keeping the bread inside, but the best place to cool a loaf is on the window sill. And the bird had promised, hadn't he? She couldn't believe that there would be no integrity, no decency at all in a creature that had such a beautiful song. Those were her thoughts as she went to the laundry to get the mop for the kitchen floor.

The sad thing is that Edith wasn't surprised at all when she re-entered the kitchen to find the same fat blackbird wallowing in her hollowed out loaf for the third time. She looked at the blackbird. The blackbird looked at her. And then it began to sing.

Sofa

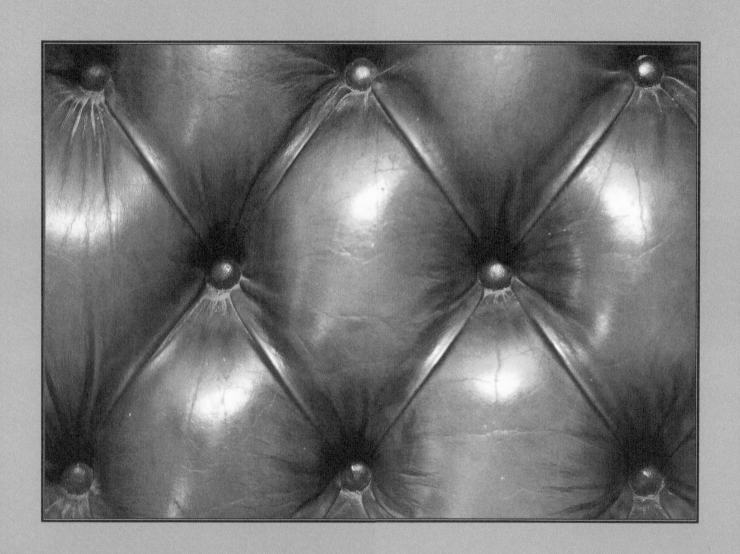

I still remember it. The girl was crying because her room-mate had told her that she would go to hell if she didn't respond to Jesus. That always sounds bad, however you say it or write it. If you don't respond to Jesus, you're going to end up in hell. You can't make that sound good. But what do you do? She'd asked her room-mate outright if that was the case. What can you say?

And there I was, in a room with a crying girl and an angry friend. They looked at me. Is it true? What do I say? What should I do? Well, I'll tell you what I did. I got flustered and scared and said nothing.

Once, when I was walking down a street in London, I walked past a homeless man. For no discernible reason he shook his fist at the sky and shouted, "There is no God!" I just lowered my head and kept walking.

We were in a McDonald's in France. A dirty-looking boy came up to me and spoke to me in French. I wasn't sure. He was either asking for some fries, or for some money for fries. I said "Non", and he walked off. When we'd finished we threw away nearly two whole portions of fries that we hadn't eaten. My French friend tells me that street gangs get boys to ask tourists for money in McDonald's so that they can buy drugs and things. I don't know about that, but I know my heart and I recognise the sound of a cockerel crowing when I hear it.

I'll be OK if I don't get my own place in heaven. I'll just sleep on Simon Peter's sofa.

By the Riverbank

Misfit sat on the riverbank, dangling her hairy legs into the water. She was really enjoying the splashing of the water on her remarkably large feet, along with the cool breeze on her decidedly ordinary face. She leant back on her arms and kicked the water aimlessly, for the sheer fun of it, much in the way that one might imagine a child doing. She sat, quite deliberately, with her back to the winding path that zigzagged its way through the green hills towards The City. In the air she could hear the tweeting of birds and wondered idly what they might be saying to each other. Perhaps they were just singing for the sheer joy of it? Maybe they were discussing the activities of the day? For all Misfit knew they could be bickering with one another. It didn't really matter to her, for all she knew was that it sounded like hope. She dived into her imagination, picturing the relationships and networks of the world of the birds.

Misfit was brought crashing back from her created universe by the sound of thudding jackboots on the path behind her. Although she kept her eyes closed and refused to turn, she allowed herself a wry smile. It had to be World. He was the only person that Misfit knew who would wear jackboots down to the riverbank. The sound of crunching grass ceased as Misfit opened her eyes and leant her head back in an effort to see behind her.

"Hello World," she remarked, the blazing sunlight forcing her to squint at the upside-down figure in her view.

World said nothing but nodded in a noncommittal greeting. Misfit shifted her body ninety degrees to get a better look at World. It meant, as she noted with a twang of annoyance, that her feet were now resting on the muddy bank rather than in the water. She leant back on one arm, freeing the other to shield her eyes from the sun. World had recently taken to wearing a kaleidoscope of garish face paint which made him, Misfit thought, look like a mime who had been on the losing side in a game of paintball. Misfit guessed that it was supposed to make World look like he was a lot of fun, but it didn't work. His words, though often eloquent and attractive, were always humourless and his eyes joyless. She noted that today he was dressed in a surgeon's smock. He changed his outfit daily and Misfit had never known anyone with a wardrobe quite as extensive as World's. The only ubiquitous elements of World's garb were the worn jackboots, the large opulent rings on his fingers and the dried blood that caked his hands. He raised one of those rust-coloured hands to his mouth and cleared his throat meaningfully. Misfit grinned again, for this was always World's way of declaring that he had something important to say.

"I think," World began slowly, "that I have finally figured out why you are called 'Misfit'. It is because you don't belong."

Misfit smiled but said nothing.

"You don't belong in the marketplace," World went on, "where idols are made, bought and sold on a daily basis; where money is carved from the bleached skulls of men, women and children, who have less value than a crate of soft drink."

"That's true," Misfit nodded. World cleared his throat again.

"Neither do you belong on the stage," he spoke ponderously, choosing his words carefully, "where the most beautiful things of your Master are cheapened and paraded like slaves through the streets of mortal culture; where drooling humans gather daily to hear terrible lies passed off as The Story."

"Also true."

"You do not belong in the barracks," World said, seeming mildly agitated by Misfit's lack of reaction, "where men and women are forced to paint murals with their own blood until they drop dead; where old men speak about your Master as though he was a four star general with a red, white and blue beard."

"Isn't it a beautiful day?" said Misfit, gazing up into the clear blue sky.

"And you certainly do not belong in the temple, where newborn gods compete with one another for their pound of flesh; where even those with whom you might have had true fellowship have been willingly imprisoned for so long that they have forgotten where the exit lies."

"I think it's perhaps the most beautiful day I've ever seen," Misfit sighed, contentedly.

"You do not belong in the town hall, where truth and lies have developed such a parasitic relationship with one another that one can no longer discern which is which; where men and women talk and talk and talk about big things while the little things remain undone." World stared into space, as though he were reciting the lines from an invisible teleprompter.

Misfit swung back round, letting her feet once more feel the embrace of the cold water.

"You do not belong in the newsroom," World said, sparing Misfit a glance as he continued, "where education is an excuse to sap the will of people who might be inclined to make a difference; where the future of nations is decided by subscription figures and the toss of a coin. You do not belong in any of these places."

Misfit hummed a tune to herself, staring into space.

"You don't belong in any of these places. That's why you are called 'Misfit'," concluded World.

"That's quite right. You're quite right," Misfit agreed.

There was silence for about half a minute. Misfit continued to splash, relishing the feel of the grass under her palms. World shuffled from foot to foot before breaking the silence.

"So where do you belong then?" he asked, curiosity getting the better of him. Misfit thought for a moment before replying, using the pause to pick up a small pebble to pitch into the water.

"I guess that I belong everywhere. And I belong right here." She smiled as the water rippled away from the pebble. "Why don't you sit with me for a while?"

Misfit sat with her back to World, waiting to see if he would take up her offer. He never had before, but maybe this time would be different. Love always hopes. About a minute passed before Misfit heard a grunt of frustration and the sound of jackboots on the path. She glanced behind her to see World stomping off towards

The City. Although it wasn't long before the tall figure vanished behind a hill, the thud of his jackboots remained for many minutes afterwards.

Eventually silence reigned. Misfit spent a pleasant half hour putting words into the mouth of fish ("Boy, am I thirsty!") before finally standing up and brushing herself down. She looked around for her shoes but couldn't seem to find them. Misfit shrugged – this wasn't the first time that she had lost a perfectly good pair of shoes and she was sure that it wouldn't be the last. She inwardly remarked on how pleasant the grass felt under her bare feet. There was always a positive side to any situation if you knew where to look. But it was time to leave.

With a sigh, she set her face like flint and headed off after World, towards The City.

The Double Tragedy of the Goblet

"**W**ould you like to see something special?"

With these words the man would bring the goblet out of its padded case. It really was a beautiful thing, its faceted crystal throwing beautiful rainbows around with abandon. The owner would show the goblet, and pass it around for admiration.

"Isn't it amazing?"

There was never disagreement. It was always amazing.

Over the years the goblet was passed from large hand to small hand to fat hand to bony hand. It was twisted and turned, admired from every angle. It was placed on surfaces and lifted up over heads. And it was always returned to the padded case.

But when it wasn't in the padded case, it was at risk. Not every hand was careful, not every observer able to conceal his envy. At first it was a scratch. Just one. Then there was another. One day there was a chip. Soon it was joined by another. The marks and scars increased. As the beauty decreased, the owner became more and more reluctant to show off the goblet. Before long, it lay imprisoned in the case, forever forgotten.

The first tragedy is that, in all that time, no-one ever drank from the goblet. No-one ever used it for its intended purpose. And then it was too late.

The second tragedy is that, in all that time, no-one ever once asked the goblet what it thought of all this.

Knock and the Door shall be Opened

I saw something very strange the other day. I was with my friends, Apathy and Easy Life, and we were walking home from our daily trip to Vanity Fair. It's a mostly delightful walk full of beautiful scenery, particularly pleasant on a summer's day. I say 'mostly' because there is one part of the walk that is certainly discomforting. At one point in the journey the road bends round to the left and leads past a tall, crooked tower. The silent building is a mishmash of broken and jagged bricks, without windows and with a single, imposing knotted wooden door in its base. It's a terribly ugly thing and all the worse for being the place where Suffering lives. We often pick up our pace when we approach this monstrosity, and once we are well past it, we relax and the jolly banter begins again.

Anyway, this particular day I felt the usual tightness in my chest as we approached the bend, but was surprised to hear a loud thudding sound. At first, I wondered if it were my own heart, thumping along in terror at the thought of the tower, but as we turned the corner I became aware that the thudding was actually being caused by a man who was hammering furiously on the door of Suffering's tower. I stopped dead in my tracks, for this was the first time that I had ever seen anyone here in this spot - let alone trying to get into the tower. I felt Apathy tug on my sleeve, impressing on me the need to pick up my pace.

"Forget it. Leave him," he spoke in his silky, well-mannered tone that is so pleasing to my ear. Easy Life nodded his agreement. I shook Apathy's hand away, unable to move on. I felt compelled to warn this stranger of the dangerous path that he trod. I'm compassionate like that.

"Excuse me," I hollered, but at first I couldn't be heard above the sound of hammering fists. I persevered (another of my wonderful character traits) until I had gained the young man's attention. He ceased his assault on the door and turned his head to look at me.

"Excuse me," I continued, "but I wouldn't do that if I were you. Suffering lives there. I think that he's best left undisturbed."

"I have to get in. I'm looking for someone and he went this way," the man explained, before resuming his bizarre action.

93

"I really wouldn't do that," I yelled, "I have never seen anyone go in there and I certainly have never seen anyone come out."

"I have to get in. I'm looking for someone and he went this way," the young man repeated, as if it were a mystical mantra that might open the door.

"You tried, but we really must be going." Easy Life tried to catch my attention. He looked worried. Apathy, standing alongside him, hopped nervously from foot to foot. I nodded. They were right. I had tried to help this fellow, but if he were so insistent on waking Suffering, then it was probably best if I left him to it. It would be a terrible thing if I were to become embroiled in this man's self-destructive action, for I had heard nothing but bad reports about Suffering and his treatment of others.

"I hope that you find your friend, but if he truly came this way then I would consider trying to find another path around," I shouted as a parting comment, hoping that the young man might reflect on my words and come to his senses. Still, it would do no good to delay my journey home. My problem is that I am always too willing to put the needs of others before myself. Apathy and Easy Life are right when they warn me that sometimes I am far too generous and need to consider my own well-being first. I resumed the journey home, and my travelling companions relaxed considerably. In fact, we all relaxed considerably as we put that infernal tower behind us. That night, I slept the peaceful sleep of the righteous.

The next morning I awoke and got myself ready for the day. At 8:06am, as per usual, Apathy and Easy Life knocked on my door and invited me to travel with them to Vanity Fair. I readily agreed, for they are my best friends. We passed Suffering's tower at 8:42am and began a brisker pace. I remembered the young man that I had come across the previous evening, but he was nowhere to be seen. The door to Suffering's tower swung open, creaking in the breeze. It seemed that the young man had received his wish after all, but could he not have at least closed the door behind him? Suffering may be a crotchety old fellow but it's just bad manners to leave someone's door wide open. Apathy and Easy Life read my thoughts, just as they always seemed to.

"Some people are just so inconsiderate," Apathy purred, glancing at the tower as we strolled past.

"Isn't it a pity that there aren't more people as thoughtful as you?" Easy Life patted my shoulder gently. My friends always know just what to say to encourage me.

"I think that if more people had friends like you two," I returned the compliment, "then the world would be a much better place."

We went our way, joking and laughing together. Loud squeals of delight travelled through the air. Some of my fellow pilgrims had already arrived at Vanity Fair, and I was eager to join them. It was good to be alive.

Hidden Things

"What's in the cupboard?" asked Pactus, raised eyebrow arching across his forehead like a curious rainbow.

"Nothing," I replied, hoping that I sounded convincing.

"You don't sound very convincing," Pactus replied.

I went on the offensive. "What's with the third degree? It's my stuff. It's none of your business."

"Hey, you're the one who invited me in."

He had me there.

"I've got you there, haven't I?"

I muttered something under my breath.

"So, what's in the cupboard?" Pactus said.

"Nothing," I repeated, sounding even less convincing than before.

Pactus reached past me and pulled open the door. Out tumbled a pile of dead sparrows.

"Did you think I didn't know?" he said.

Un Dieu Défini est un Dieu Fini

definitely
2 certainly
yes, certainly.
definition
a statement
2 a the
(esp. of an
or on a
outline

We had a man over for dinner the other day. I invited him in, took his coat, offered him a drink – all the stuff that a good host is supposed to do. When it was time for dinner, I led him over to the table.

"I thought you could sit here, next to my youngest daughter," I explained.

He looked confused.

"Where?"

"Next to Imogen. Here," I repeated.

"What? In the high chair?" He was incredulous.

I had gone to a lot of trouble for him. I had sourced a second high chair for Imogen, and given him hers. He was the guest. He should have the best one. I had even provided a really nice bib. It was one of those flexible plastic ones. Comfortable, without sacrificing its ability to catch stray food. I thought he'd appreciate it, but apparently not.

"I'm not sitting in a high chair for a meal!" he exclaimed.

"My wife told me that you were the youngest child in your family."

"And?" he asked.

I looked at him, and then at my youngest daughter, and then back at him.

"Youngest child. I have one of those. She sits in a high chair and eats with a bib. Youngest child. Young. Child."

"I'm forty-seven and I'm a particle physicist. I'm not sitting in a high chair or wearing a bib."

Words are tricky things. We always think we know what they mean to everyone else. The French have a saying: A god who is defined is a god who is finished.

Lunchtime

I paid for my lunch and moved to the seating area, looking for a place to sit and enjoy my meal. As I wandered along I noticed a man, who had both a fully loaded tray and a look of anguish.

"What's wrong?" I asked him.

"I don't know which table to sit at, and my food is getting cold," he responded, genuinely distressed.

Well, it hardly seemed a matter of life or death to me, but it was clearly important to this fellow. I thought I'd help him out by doing a bit of research on his behalf.

I picked a table that looked like it would be fun to sit at. There was one empty seat left. At the head of the table sat a distinguished looking gentleman dressed in a military uniform, sharing a joke with one of his neighbours, who appeared to be a priest.

"Excuse me," I interrupted, "do you have room for one more? For that guy over there?"

The head of the table looked intently at the worried man, and then grinned.

"For him? Of course!"

"Great. Thanks. I'll let him know. Oh, by the way – what's your name?"

"My name is Dogma," said the man, lifting a great spoon of soup into his mouth.

That seemed easy. But I thought that maybe I should get a second opinion, just in case the man didn't actually want to sit at that table. After all, it looked like a fun place to be, but it also seemed a bit crowded. Maybe this guy was after a more quiet, reflective experience. I spotted another table, where there were plenty of empty chairs.

In fact, at this table there was just one space taken. The lone figure looked tired and weary, and ate his small meal slowly. As I got closer to him, I noticed that he had a swollen, blackened eye, and a broken nose. A scar ran down his face, from the length of one ear to just short of his mouth, but his eyes were filled with something that you might call joy.

"Excuse me," I asked, "but would you mind if that guy over there sat with you?"

"Not at all. I'd be happy for him to join me," the broken figure said, smiling.

"OK. Well, what's your name?" I added.

"My name is Love," came the response.

I wondered back over to the man, who was still pacing and looking agitated.

"Look, I've checked it out. You can sit at that table, or at that table. They've both got room for you," I explained.

"Thank you. But which one should I sit at?"

"What's your name?" I asked.

"Faith."

"Well, then you'd better choose carefully," I said.

Urges to be Killed (Two)

After such a long time in the darkness, to pull myself up a rope, clamber out of a crack in the ground and find myself standing in the sunlight thrilled me in a way that I couldn't remember having felt before. It was like clawing my way out of a grave. I looked around, but there was no sign of the Stranger who had gotten me into this mess.

I took in my surroundings. I was standing on the peak of a hill; before me a beautiful panoramic view of the countryside. It had been a long time since I had ventured outside of my city, and I had forgotten how many wonderful things could be found in the outside world. I decided that it would do me good to sit here on this hill for a while, and just enjoy my freedom.

Every second that passed seemed like a blessing. To rest and enjoy life; it had been so long since I had allowed myself that privilege. Previously, I'd always had things to do and responsibilities to fulfil. As I sat in peace, the seconds blurred into days, and I began to lose track of time. But I didn't care.

One day, I noticed a thin black line on the horizon. It was a curiosity, but nothing more, until the following day when I noticed that the line was a bit thicker than it had been the day before. Not by much, just a little, but it was definitely thicker. The next day, it was bigger still. I realised that, whatever it was, it was moving towards me. As the days rolled past, that thin line became thicker and thicker as it drew nearer and nearer, and eventually it began to resemble a jagged, threatening skyline. A nagging feeling took root in my soul; the feeling that all was not well. The peace I had been experiencing faded away like mist.

Before long I could tell that the jagged skyline was actually formed by a gathering of banners and spears. The black line advancing towards me from the horizon was an army, and instinctively I knew that it was coming for me. I hurriedly took stock of my memories. Was it the army of a rival king? Some pretender I had snubbed? Was it just some arbitrary force of marauders, looking for prey? Whoever they were, I knew that they were coming for me and my hilltop paradise. It was then that I noticed, in my panicked pacing, the rocks around me.

The next days were a blur. No peace, because I moved in terror, shifting those rocks into some kind of fortification. It took all my strength and consumed all my hours, but the army was marching day and night at a relentless pace. After the working was done, I had constructed a rocky palisade at the peak of my hill. A barrier that would surely hold off the approaching force. My peace returned. I was safe. I was secure. And I slept.

I was woken by a loud cough beside me. I was slow to respond, for surely it couldn't be the army. Even if they had reached me, I was safe behind my wall. Anyway, they had spears, not dry throats. The cough repeated. I sat up and rubbed my eyes, and at my feet stood a familiar figure.

"Been busy, have we?" the Stranger inquired.

"How did you get in?" I demanded to know, my irritation plain. I could overlook the fact that the Stranger was responsible for my trouble, but now he was disturbing my restful slumber and that was just rude.

"How did I get in? What do you mean?" he responded.

"Through my barrier. Past my wall," I explained, as though speaking to a dimwit.

"I just walked in. Round the side."

That nagging feeling resurfaced. The peace slipped away once again.

"What do you mean?" I was afraid of the answer.

"Your barrier doesn't even go round the whole hill. It's not even a foot high. This isn't even a garden wall, let alone a castle wall. What's it for?"

"To keep out the army." I pointed to the horizon. The marching troops were ever so close now and I could begin to make out the individual figures in each rank. There were hundreds of them, probably thousands.

"This wall won't work." The Stranger shook his head.

"It will. It will protect me," I protested.

"No, it won't. Watch this."

The Stranger lashed out with his foot and kicked the bottom of my wall. Two large stones tumbled from the top. I was enraged.

"Why do you always have to be so negative? Why can't you just leave me alone?"

"Because sometimes being right is the kindest thing," the Stranger said, unmoved.

"Leave me alone. Leave me alone for the army to come up here, knock through my wall and kill me." I threw myself to the ground.

The Stranger grabbed me by my arm and pulled me to my feet. He was surprisingly strong.

"You can't hide from this army. Not behind your wall. But you don't have to die either. There is a third way," he explained as he set me on my feet.

"What's that?"

"You fight," the Stranger said, and held something out to me. It was the hilt of a sword.

"I'll be slaughtered!" I objected.

"You won't be alone," replied the Stranger, and I noticed – for the first time – that he wore a sword at his side.

"Instead of one against the horde, it would be two? That ends the same way."

"You're forgetting," he said, "what happened the last time someone tried to kill me."

I looked at my wall. Before it had seemed impassable, something that would truly protect me. Now I saw a small pile of rocks that wouldn't even delay a determined badger.

"Even after what happened in the city, you still don't believe me?" the Stranger wondered. It was a question, but not an accusation.

I kicked out at my wall, once, twice, three times, and it crumbled before me. With a sigh, I took the blade that the Stranger had offered, and the two of us turned to meet the approaching army.

Pride

It was there when I looked in the mirror again. Every morning it was the same. I'd roll out of bed, drag myself to the bathroom, gaze at my own reflection, and there it was. The same place as always. Sitting on my shoulder, yellow lips curled back revealing a set of sharp needles.

It had been the same for years. Looking in the mirror each day to see it perched there, like a hideous parrot, its talons clutching my shoulder and its malevolent glare. I knew what it was. It was Pride.

I had tried to get rid of it many times, in many different ways. Once I had attempted to rid myself of Pride by force. It dug its vicious claws in and snapped at my hand with cruel teeth. I harmed myself more than I harmed it.

Another time I tried to starve it. I thought it was working quite well, until I glanced in the mirror the following day and saw it once more, unmoved and grinning, looking as well-fed as normal.

I tried to deny it, to hide its ugliness. I did everything I could to draw attention away from it. I dressed to cover it. I refused to acknowledge it. But every morning, there it was. It didn't help, no more than it would to hide the symptoms of a disease and expect that to make you well.

I was tired, angry and discouraged. It was time to seek out some help. I went to visit the wisest man that I knew and shared my problem. I told him of this horrible thing, Pride, that sat on my shoulder and was the first thing I saw; the only thing that I saw, it's ugly, smug face, every morning when I got up and looked in the mirror.

The wise man produced a wan smile and gently shook his head.

"Stop looking in the mirror," he said.

Death

Death, the Stealer of Souls, sat on the precipice overlooking the great cities of all the nations. His legs draped over the side, dangling over the chasm that was so deep that the bottom was merely a suggestion rather than a reality. The wind was so strong that it would have torn his hood back from his head, were he not the personification of an unstoppable, immovable force that wind and rain and lightning could only aspire to. If the gale had been able to fulfil its intentions then it would have revealed only an empty space where a head should be. More than a space, in fact, but rather an absolute space. Not just the absence of a head, but an overwhelming emptiness that would have swallowed up anything that you tried to place there, so that the vacancy was all that remained. The hooded cranium rested casually on a pale, glowing hand.

"All this is mine." He gestured vaguely at the cities with his other arm, which then returned to his side. He gently caressed the rough and stony ground he sat on as he continued.

"All of these cities pay tribute to me. None may refuse, for they chose me. You know what they're like. Ardent defenders of their free will. They chose me as their king, and none may refuse my demands and my requests. They serve me, willingly or unwillingly, and I claim each and every one of them."

You could be listening for the voice very hard and not hear it. You could desperately be trying to ignore its dry, brittle whisper, but still hear it louder than church bells. Death never raised his voice. He didn't need to. When he called, none could refuse. When he spoke, all heeded. He only spoke when he needed to, and he only spoke to those whom he wished to call. No-one else would hear him. Not yet, at least.

"All mine," he repeated.

If you had been watching this scene from afar you would have been forgiven for thinking that Death was alone. It became apparent that this was not the case. The darkness beside him shifted as a reclining figure moved into a more comfortable position. Death stared past the horizon into other worlds, refusing to even glance in the direction of his companion. The man next to Death nodded slowly, his features still shrouded by the absence of light. Death gestured again.

"A few, of course, are pleased to see me. Others are not so keen. They try to outwit me, to fool me. They don't understand. They cannot beat me at the game I invented, especially as they do not even know the rules. They chose me, and now I make the choices. Sometimes I take the young, sometimes the old. But I always take those whom I choose."

The voice sounded old, but not old as we might think it. Not *old* as in weak and frail, but rather timeless. Just because an oak tree is *old*, it doesn't mean that it is not strong. It formed gentle laughter now, a horrible grinding sound as though his lungs were full of gravel.

"They wonder. They wonder. They can't understand." Death's voice sounded more urgent and triumphant than before.

"Some do understand."

The man reclining next to Death spoke for the first time. His voice was nothing special, but next to Death's it sounded like the very chimes from the bells of the heavenly Jerusalem. Death's posture expressed his displeasure.

"What?" he hissed.

"Some understand. Some see you for what you are. *You* of all people should know that." The figure turned his head to face Death.

Death nodded, an action which seemed to take centuries, his gaze fixed rigidly on the horizon.

"*Some* understand me, maybe. But how many? What are a handful of grains of sand compared to the beach?"

The man chuckled.

"Very poetic."

Death shrugged. The man continued, looking out over the cities.

"They defy you."

"Some honour me. I have songs written about me, books written for me, films and plays performed on my behalf. Many, many more than you do, my friend."

Anyone who heard the voice couldn't have helped but notice that the words 'my friend' were spoken with no sincerity. It was true that these two were not friends, but bitter enemies. Not just enemies, but opposites.

"That may be," the man said, non-committedly.

"I am the one with the choice. They wonder why a man will live to ninety, despite the fact that he smokes fifty cigarettes a day and lives a life of utter debauchery, and yet why a child of five may heed my call. They call it 'luck', or 'one of those things'. They try to convince themselves that there are ways of cheating me. Ways to extend their days. The truth is that there is no way. They live in fear of the fact that I could beckon them any time I choose, regardless of status and lifestyle. The man who doesn't smoke can be the victim of a road accident, or maybe he'll get lung cancer anyway. It is up to me."

If you could have seen the face of the man next to Death, you would have seen him raise his eyebrows.

"Really? Your choice?" he said innocently. Death radiated hatred, but said nothing. He hated this man more than any of the other Children of Adam.

"Even you, Death, have your master."

"My Father?"

"Not your father. Mine," the man said.

Death snorted.

"My master is He? I do not see Him prevent me working. Every day provides me with new tributes and rewards. He has never stopped me."

Death threw his hands in the air. Tradition usually armed death with a scythe to reap his victims with, yet he needed nothing but his hands to collect the harvest of souls. They were cruel hands, strong and harsh. Death turned his head for the first time and regarded his companion with his eyeless vision. He slowly lifted his arm and pointed an accusing finger. It was a cruel finger.

"He even let me have you." Mocking laughter punctuated Death's words.

"For a while," the man added, nodding nonetheless.

Death turned his attention back to the landscape and was silent. Neither spoke for some time. It could have been seconds, it could have been aeons. Death's companion stood up, the darkness following him as he moved.

"Yes, for a while I was yours. For a short time you had me. You rejoiced on that day, as did your father. You rejoiced. You rejoice no longer."

More time passed. Death sat and stared at his realms, drumming his fingers on the ground. His companion stared at him, arms folded. Slowly Death turned to look up at the man, but the rebuke he was going to offer died on his lips as the man spoke again.

"You reap the souls of mankind. You wallow in them as a pig may wallow in mud, and you call them your 'tribute' and your 'wages'. They are not yours."

Death began to reply.

"Be silent! You may take them all, but you cannot keep them. There are many, many grains of sand on your beach that I call 'brother' or 'sister'. More than a mere handful. You are not eternal and even you too will pass. You know this to be true!" the figure spoke angrily. He raised his arms and tilted his head back, his robe and hair wildly blowing in the wind, and with a shouted word of command the darkness fell from around him revealing his majesty.

"You took me, but you could not keep me. You snatched my soul from the Cross like a thirsty man gulping water, and you buried me under the earth. You laughed and sneered and spat and howled and jeered, yet I live!"

The wind fell silent as the Lord of Creation spoke. The ground beneath Death shook and trembled and groaned. Glory surrounded the man as a rumble of thunder from the skies shook the foundations of the great cities. The darkness swirled and forks of lightning lit the clouds like great lights.

"They do not want you!" Death howled, jumping to his feet and shaking his fists at the Lamb of God. He screamed above the thunder in a voice more terrifying than anything that had ever been heard. "They chose me! They helped me claim you! You cannot stop me! You cannot beat me! You can—" Death's words died in his throat as the Saviour regarded him with narrowed eyes.

He slowly lowered his hands from the sky and held them out to Death, so that he could see the ragged crimson wounds that still looked so tender and painful.

"But I already have," Jesus said softly.

THE END?

Are you still listening?

Do you have time for one last story?

Once upon a time, Man and Woman lived in a wonderful garden with the God who had created them. Every day they would walk with Him through their amazing world. His voice, the voice that had called everything they knew into being, was the only voice in their world. But one day they met a serpent, and the serpent brought with it another voice; a voice that set itself against the Creator.

"He told us that it was good," said the Man and the Woman.

"But could it be better?" asked the serpent.

"He has given us everything that we need," said the Man and Woman.

"Are you sure?" asked the serpent.

The Man and Woman had to choose who to believe, and they made a bad choice. Since that time, men and women have found that the voice of God is now just one voice amongst the many.

But the story doesn't end there. Many years passed and then there was a man who heard God calling his name. This man had the same choice as the Man and the Woman. Would he listen or not?

"What do you want of me?" asked Abram.

"I want you to go," replied God. Abram went, and in doing so he became a different person. He became Abraham.

In the years that followed, there were men and women who listened to the voice of God, and men and women who listened to other voices.

Eventually along came one who made his whole life revolve around listening to the voice of God. He had a different name for God, however. He called Him 'Father'. Everywhere that this man walked, he made sure that he was walking with his Father. In the wilderness; by the lake in Galilee; on the Temple Mount; in a garden called Gethsemane and on a hill called Golgotha, wherever he went, his Father's voice was the only voice He listened to. He said, "I can do nothing except what I see my Father doing."

Jesus taught his followers that to have seen him was to have seen the Father, and by extension, that to have heard him was to have heard the Father. One day Jesus had to leave his followers, but he didn't leave them alone. He sent them the Comforter. Jesus, the God With Us, sent the Holy Spirit, the God In Us. To this very day, wherever the followers of Jesus go, God goes with them, and like the Man and Woman at the beginning of the story they can hear God, if they listen carefully, because they carry the voice of God with them.

Listen. The story goes on.

"The Sovereign LORD has given me an instructed tongue, to know the word that sustains the weary.

He wakens me morning by morning, wakens my ear to listen like one being taught.

The Sovereign LORD has opened my ears, and I have not been rebellious; I have not drawn back."

Isaiah 50:4-5

ABOUT THE AUTHOR

James has had a variety of interesting learning experiences in his life, some from being a Baptist minister in the UK and then some from being a member of Cornerstone Community, a mission and discipleship community in Australia. He fancies himself as something of a storyteller, and this book is his first attempt to put some of the things he's learnt into words. James currently lives in Canterbury with his wife and five (yes, five) children.

"...for my hope is in you all day long."

Lightning Source UK Ltd.
Milton Keynes UK
UKOW07f1804020516

273409UK00005B/13/P